THE ROYAL DRUM

An Ashanti Tale

retold by Mary Dixon Lake

illustrated by Carol O'Malia

A Note About the Story
This tale is from the Ashanti Tribe of Ghana. Their famous folklore spider, Anansi, is also called Kwaku Anansi, Nansii, or sometimes Father Spider. He is known for his tricks, which can get him into trouble, but he also likes to help his friends.

To my mother, Georgia Butts Dixon, and in
remembrance of my father, Mitchell Dixon
                              —M. L. D.

For Andrew Fyffe
          —C. O'M.

The illustrations for this book were done in oil paint;
the rebus characters were created on scratchboard.

Text copyright © 1996 by Mary Dixon Lake
Illustrations copyright © 1996 by Carol O'Malia

For information contact:
MONDO Publishing
One Plaza Road
Greenvale, New York 11548

Printed in Hong Kong

96 97 98 99 00 01   9 8 7 6 5 4 3 2 1

Designed by Edward Miller
Production by Our House

Library of Congress Cataloging-in-Publication Data

Lake, Mary Dixon.
    The Royal Drum: An Ashanti Tale / Mary Dixon Lake ; illustrated by Carol O/Malia
        p.   cm.
Summary: All the animals, except the lazy Monkey, work to make a drum for the King of the Jungle,
but Anansi makes certain that Monkey ends up with the hardest job of all.
    ISBN 1-57255-140-2 (hc) ISBN 1-57255-125-9 (pbk) ISBN 1-57255-126-7 (big book)

    [1. Ashanti (African people)–Folklore. 2.Folklore–Ghana.] I. O'Malia, Carol, ill. II. Title.   PZ8.1.L96Ro   1996
398.2´09667´04252987—dc20   95-33612

A Key to Rebus Characters

Anansi

Giraffe

King

Antelope

Elephant

Hippo

Leopard

Drum

Jackel

Monkey

One day, the 🦁 called a meeting.

   "A meeting, a meeting! The 🦁 calls a meeting."

   The messengers spread the news. All the animals heard the cry.

"Hurry, hurry," they said, as they set out at great speed. It took many days before they finally reached the King's palace.

"Thank you for coming," the 🦁 said, "for I need your help. We have a big problem."

"Problem?" trumpeted 🐘 .

"Problem?" whispered 🦒 .

"Problem?" growled 🐺 .

"Yes, yes!" cried the  . "And who can

solve it? For too many days pass before we

come together!"

"Yes, too many," agreed  .

"Too, too many," said  .

"Far too many," answered  .

"We must make a change," said the  .

"Yes, a change," said  .

"A definite change," agreed  .

"Indeed a change," replied  .

"We must find a way to send a message

immediately," the  said.

stepped up, *pip-pip-pip-pip, pip, pip, pip.*

He had been listening to everything. He was

counselor to the . After thinking

carefully, he said, "What we need is a royal .

Its sound will travel everywhere. Then we

will all come at once."

"This is wonderful," exclaimed .

"Brilliant," remarked .

"Wise," said .

"It shall be done," ordered the .

The animals quickly began working. Each took a turn in the making of the royal . found a log in the jungle and carried it, *mun, mun, mun.* trimmed the branches, *kut-zu, kut-zu, kut-zu.* Termites hollowed it out and carved it, *chun, chun, chat-wa-chat-wa, chun, chun, chun.*

Everyone was busy, busy, busy. That is, everyone except . While all the animals worked, slept, *huh-za, huh-za,* in a shady spot.

When the animals finished work, they sang, "*OO, oo, OO-oo-OO, OO, oo,* we are so-o-o tired." joined in and sang of his tiredness, too.

At last, the was ready, and this was the sound it made:

Kra-ka-ka-hi,

kee-yop, kee-yop,

Kra-ka-ka-hi,

kee-yop, kee-yop.

The animals hopped on one foot, then on the other.

"*Yo, yo, yo,*" cried the . "Bring the

to my palace."

"Who shall carry the ?" asked .

The was very heavy and large. The

distance was too far, too far. No one wanted

to carry the .

 said, " shall have the honor,

for she is the most graceful."

"No," said , " should carry it, for

he is so fast."

"Why, is strong and should do it,"

replied . Each animal named another to

carry the .

Finally, 🕷 said, "No one wants to carry the 🥁. I think the one who is most lazy should carry it."

"Yes, yes," agreed the 🦁. "What a fine idea!"

All the animals looked at each other. "Who is the lazy one?" each animal thought. One by one, each animal looked at 🐒.

🐒 jumped and hopped, jumped and hopped. All the animals were looking at him.

"*Puh!*" 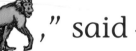 said. "I will never, never carry

the 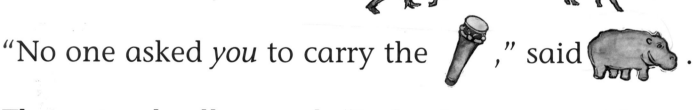. Never, and that is all I will say!"

The animals laughed, *kye, kye, kye.*

"No one called *your* name, 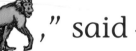," said 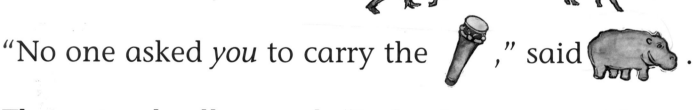.

"No one asked *you* to carry the 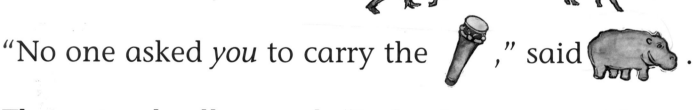," said 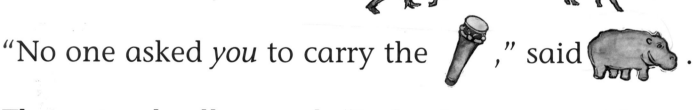.

The animals all agreed, "Indeed, no one said

a word to you."

"I will not, I will not, carry the ,"  cried again and stamped his feet. The animals still laughed, *kye, kye, kye.*

 told the , "No one called 's name. Everyone was thinking, Who is lazy, lazy, lazy? They did not say. But  *knew.* He told them he will not carry the . He, then, is the laziest of all."

And so, to take the  from the jungle to the palace of the , it was who carried it.